Originally published as *Voor elkaar*
in Belgium and the Netherlands by Clavis Uitgeverij, 2022
English translation from the Dutch by Clavis Publishing Inc., New York

Visit us on the Web at www.clavis-publishing.com.

Little Book of Caring written and illustrated by Francesca Pirrone

ISBN 978-1-60537-785-8

This book was printed in March 2022 at Graspo CZ, a.s.,
Pod Šternberkem 324, 76302 Zlín, Czech Republic.

First Edition
10 9 8 7 6 5 4 3 2 1

Clavis Publishing supports the First Amendment and celebrates the right to read.

Francesca Pirrone

Little Book of Caring

Clavis

NEW YORK

It's easy to show you care . . .

Just say good morning!

Say I'm sorry.

Be helpful.

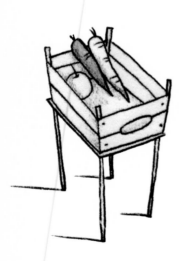

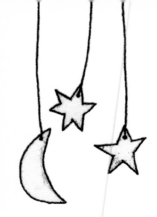

Tidy up.

Listen.

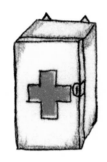

Look after.

Practice self-care.

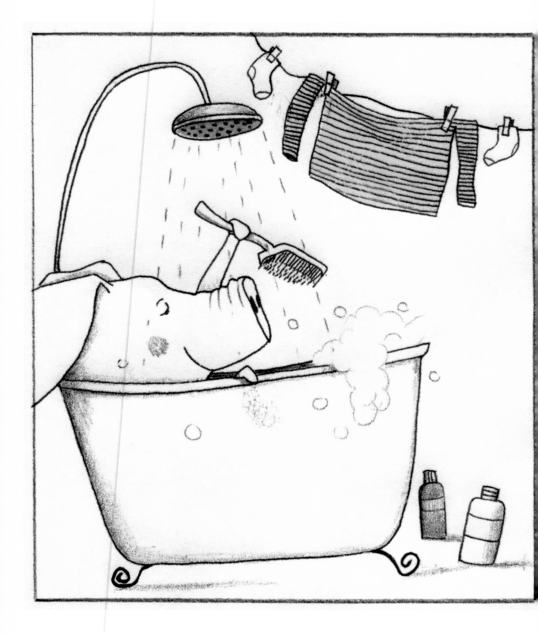

Share what you don't need anymore.

Be welcoming.

Recycle.

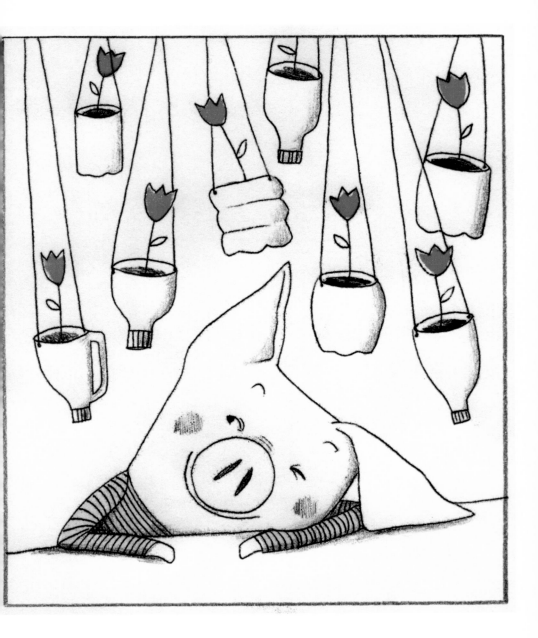

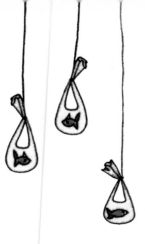

Think of someone else's feelings.

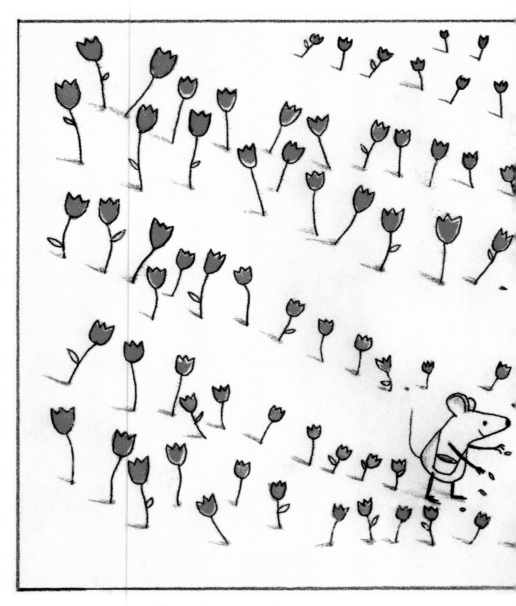

Care for the little things . . .

and they'll grow big.